UnitedHealthcare
Children's Foundation®

ISBN: 978-0-9897937-3-5

Manufactured in the United States of America. First Edition.

Publisher: UHCCF/Adventure
Author: Meg Cadts and UHCCF
Illustrator: Samantha Fitch
Contact: UnitedHealthcare Children's Foundation

UnitedHealthcare Children's Foundation
PO Box 41 | Minneapolis, MN 55440-0041

1-855-MY-UHCCF
1-855-698-4223
uhccf.org

Oliver & Hope's™

SUPERHERO SATURDAY

Written By Meg Cadts

Illustrated By Samantha Fitch

"Being a bear is pretty fun,"
Oliver said with a smile.
"But pretending to be a
SUPERHERO BEAR
is twice as fun."

His friends, Hope the butterfly
and Charlotte the fox, agreed.
So they put on their capes and
became superheroes. Just for today.

Oliver imagined he could fly, like Hope.

And Hope pretended she was strong, like Oliver.

"I'm going to be the world's smartest superhero!"
Charlotte said proudly. She was always curious about the world and loved helping her friends solve tricky problems.

Racing through the woods, the three friends were ready to save the world from danger (as long as they got back in time for dinner).

Before long, Oliver, Hope and Charlotte came upon a strange cave at the edge of a creek.

"That cave looks just like a whale," said Charlotte.
Oliver and Hope couldn't really see a whale, but after squinting their eyes and stretching their imaginations, the friends all pretended they were heroes at sea.

"Look out!"

shouted Oliver. "That humpback whale is about to swallow a pirate ship. Quick, let's save it!"

"I know what to do," said Charlotte, using her superhero aim to toss a rope right into the whale's huge mouth.

They worked together to pull the pirate ship to safety. It didn't even matter that the ship was really just an old log. The friends were too busy being heroes to worry about little details like that.

Back on the trail, Oliver, Hope and Charlotte were on the lookout
for their next big adventure. And it didn't take long...

"Look, up in the tree!" cried Oliver.
"We've got to rescue that balloon."

Hope wondered how her friends would reach the balloon since
they didn't have wings. But then she remembered it was simply
their imaginations that needed to take flight.

The friends imagined the balloon was in a **race around the world.**
They needed their special powers to set it free.

Charlotte knew what to do.
"I'll steer it away from the branches.
Oliver, you can help push us out.
Hope, you untangle the rope!"

The balloon would soon be back in the race with its other flying friends.

"Wow, pretending to be a superhero is **tough work**," thought Hope. "How do real superheroes make it look so easy?" she wondered.

To their surprise, they found their friends Millie the barn owl and Chewie the English bulldog. Chewie was stuck in a thick patch of soupy, soggy mud.

"THANK GOODNESS YOU CHAPS ARRIVED!" Chewie cheered.
"Hoo-hoo... hooray!" hooted Millie. She was happy to see her friends, but still wasn't sure how they'd get Chewie out of the mud.

Hope looked on nervously and thought,
"We're really good at pretending to be superheroes.
But now it looks like we **REALLY** need to save the day."

Oliver tried to reach Chewie,
but he was too far away.

Then Charlotte tried tiptoeing closer to Chewie.
"Oh, yuck!" she cried,
before almost getting stuck in the mud herself.
Things weren't looking too good.

Just then, Charlotte had an idea.

"Hope, if you and Millie work together, you'll be able to reach Chewie!"

Hope was nervous.
But, to her surprise, as she
gently landed next to Millie, her tiny
body and wings added just enough
weight to make the branch bend
down so Chewie could reach it.

"I'M Free!" Chewie shouted.
"Jolly good work, mates. You are my heroes."

"Welcome to the superhero team!"
Charlotte said, handing Chewie his very own cape.
"Now you can fly like Hope, Millie and the rest of us," she said with a wink.

Chewie knew exactly what to do next.
But he was going to need a little help from his friends...

The five friends sprung into action, using their imaginary powers
to overcome their imaginary foe.

After rescuing the **pirate ship**, freeing the **hot air balloon** and battling
the **evil mud monster**, the friends began their journey back home,
ready to save the world from anything that stood in their way...
as long as they got home in time for dinner, of course.

They knew More adventures would be
coming their way soon.

Stories that inspire.

You can help us write the next chapter.

The Oliver & Hope™ series tells stories of adventure, curiosity and perseverance. Stories of hope and imagination. And, in many ways, these same elements help guide the mission of the UnitedHealthcare Children's Foundation (UHCCF), a 501(c)(3) charitable organization. UHCCF supports the UnitedHealth Group's mission to "help people live healthier lives" and aligns under the enterprise values of Integrity, Compassion, Relationships, Innovation and Performance.

Each year, UHCCF offers grants to help children gain access to medically-related services that are not covered, or not fully covered, by their parents' commercial health insurance plan. It is through these grants — and the shared commitment of our staff, volunteers, sponsors and recipients — that truly inspiring stories unfold.

The best part is you can be a part of these stories, which continue to write new chapters each year. If you know a family that could benefit from a UHCCF medical grant, you can help make an introduction. And, if you are able to offer your time or resources, we have many ways for you to get involved. Even the smallest contribution can help make a major impact in the lives of the families we work with.

Visit UHCCF.org today and become part of the story.

UHCCF.org | 1-855-MY-UHCCF | 1-855-698-4223

UnitedHealthcare Children's Foundation
PO Box 41 | Minneapolis, MN 55440-0041